GET IN THE GAME
FACE-OFF

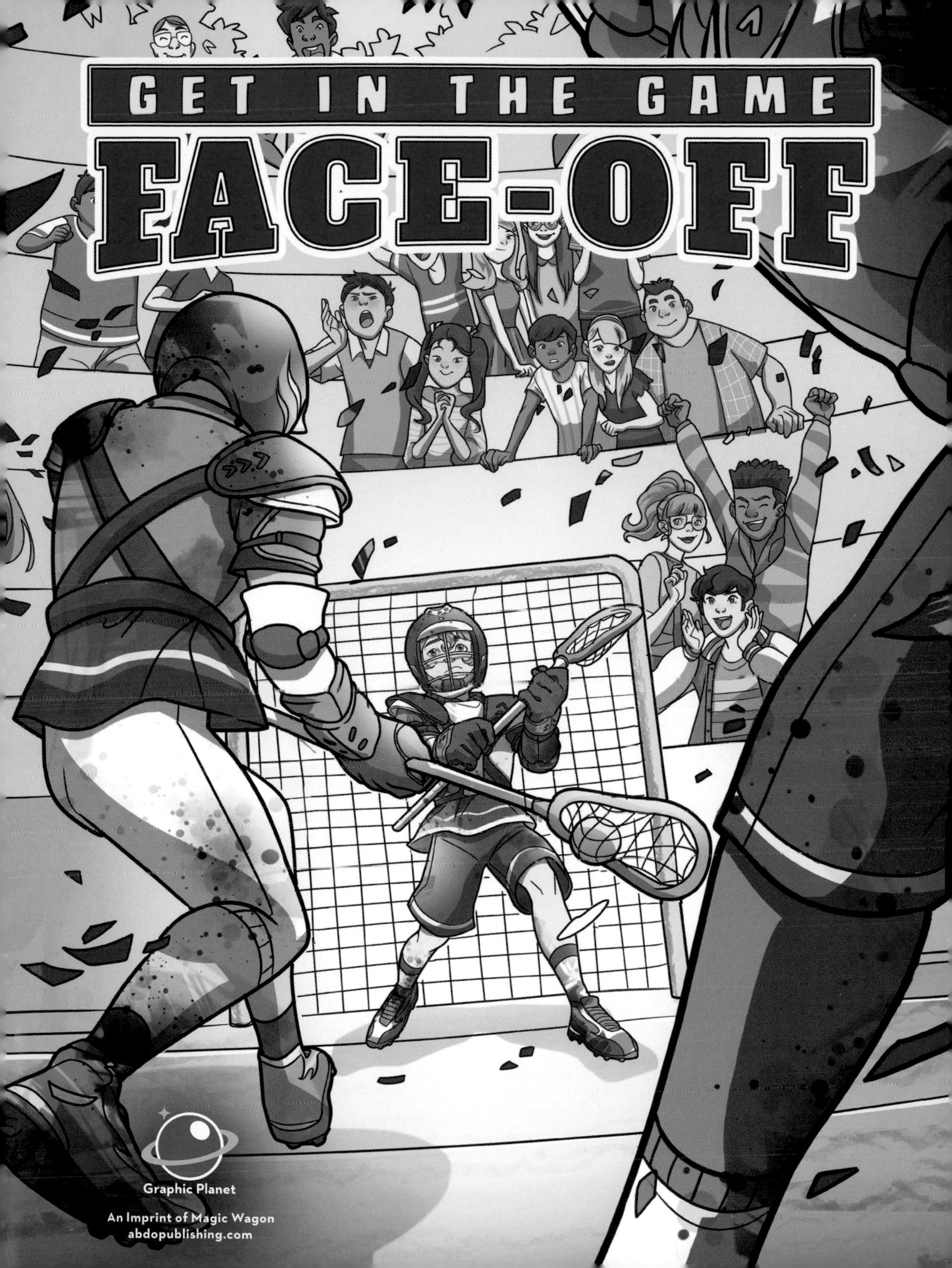

Graphic Planet

An Imprint of Magic Wagon
abdopublishing.com

abdopublishing.com

Published by Magic Wagon, a division of ABDO, PO Box 398166, Minneapolis, Minnesota 55439.
Copyright © 2019 by Abdo Consulting Group, Inc. International copyrights reserved in all countries.
No part of this book may be reproduced in any form without written permission from the publisher.
Graphic Planet™ is a trademark and logo of Magic Wagon.

Printed in the United States of America, North Mankato, Minnesota.
052018
092018

Written by David Lawrence
Ancillaries written by Bill Yu
Pencils by Paola Amormino
Inks by Renato Siragusa
Colored by Tiziana Musmeci
Lettered by Kathryn S. Renta
Card Illustrations by Emanuele Cardillo and Gabriele Cracolici (Grafimated)
Layout and design by Pejee Calanog of Glass House Graphics and Christina Doffing of ABDO
Editorial supervision by David Campiti
Edited by Giovanni Spadaro (Grafimated Cartoon)
Packaged by Glass House Graphics
Art Directed by Candice Keimig
Editorial Support by Tamara L. Britton

Library of Congress Control Number: 2018932634

Publisher's Cataloging-in-Publication Data

Names: Lawrence, David, author. | Amormino, Paola, illustrator. | Siragusa, Renato, illustrator.
Title: Face-off / by David Lawrence; illustrated by Paola Amormino and Renato Siragusa.
Description: Minneapolis, Minnesota : Magic Wagon, 2019. | Series: Get in the game
Summary: Artie Lieberman tries out for Peabody's lacrosse team. He is excited to make the team. But
  when he is bullied by a group of bigger boys, he's not sure he wants to keep playing. Can he stand up
  to the bullies? Is it even worth it?
Identifiers: ISBN 9781532132957 (lib.bdg.) | ISBN 9781532133091 (ebook) |
  ISBN 9781532133169 (Read-to-me ebook)
Subjects: LCSH: Lacrosse--Juvenile fiction. | Bullying--Juvenile fiction. | Sports teams--Juvenile fiction. |
  Self-reliance in adolescence--Juvenile fiction. | Graphic novels--Juvenile fiction.
Classification: DDC 741.5--dc2

CONTENTS

FACE-OFF

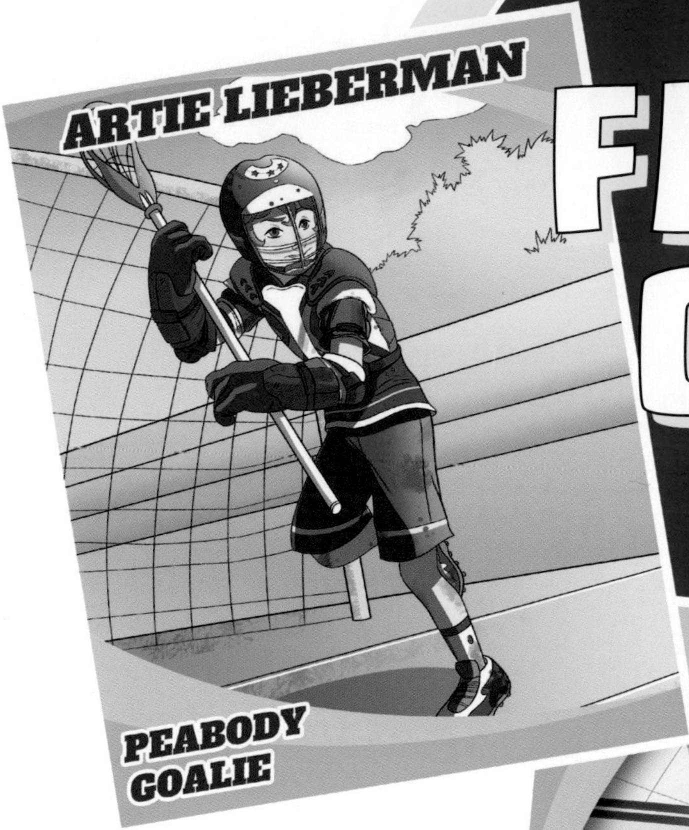
ARTIE LIEBERMAN
PEABODY
GOALIE

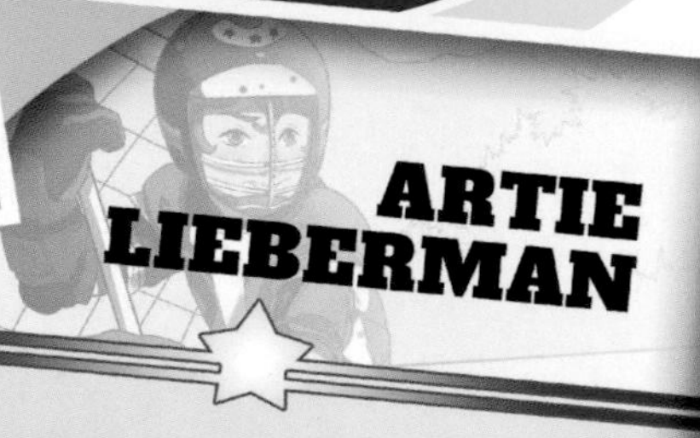
ARTIE
LIEBERMAN

Artie Lieberman, Goalie #35

Scrappy Artie Lieberman is the heart of Peabody's fledgling lacrosse team. His hard work and commitment is an inspiration to his teammates. His favorite athlete is professional wrestler Bill Goldberg.

RECORD

GAMES	MINUTES	SHOTS	SAVES	PCT	W/L
8	320	141	75	531	4-4

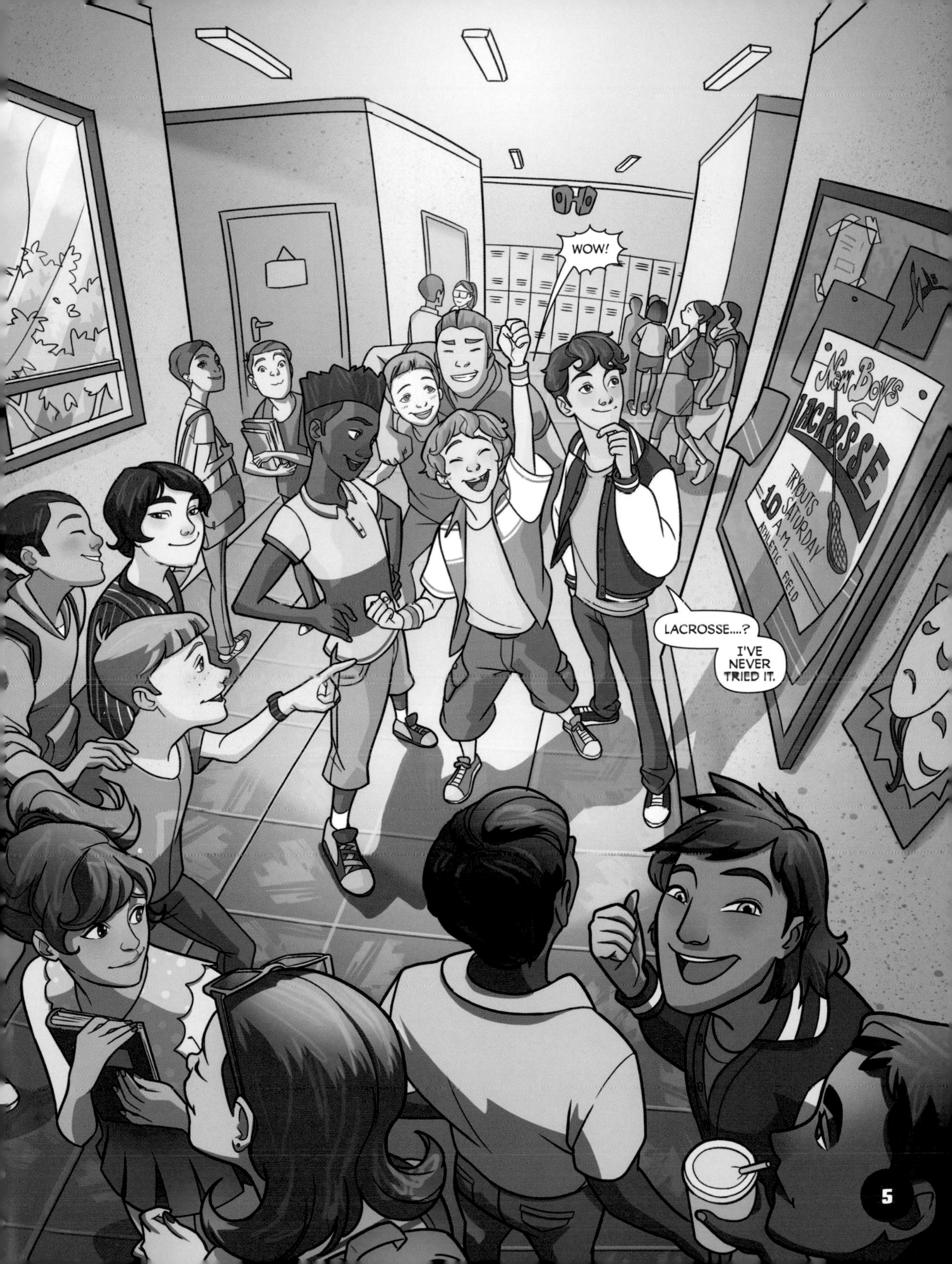
WOW!
New Boys
LACROSSE
TRYOUTS SATURDAY
10 A.M.
ATHLETIC FIELD
LACROSSE....?
I'VE NEVER TRIED IT.

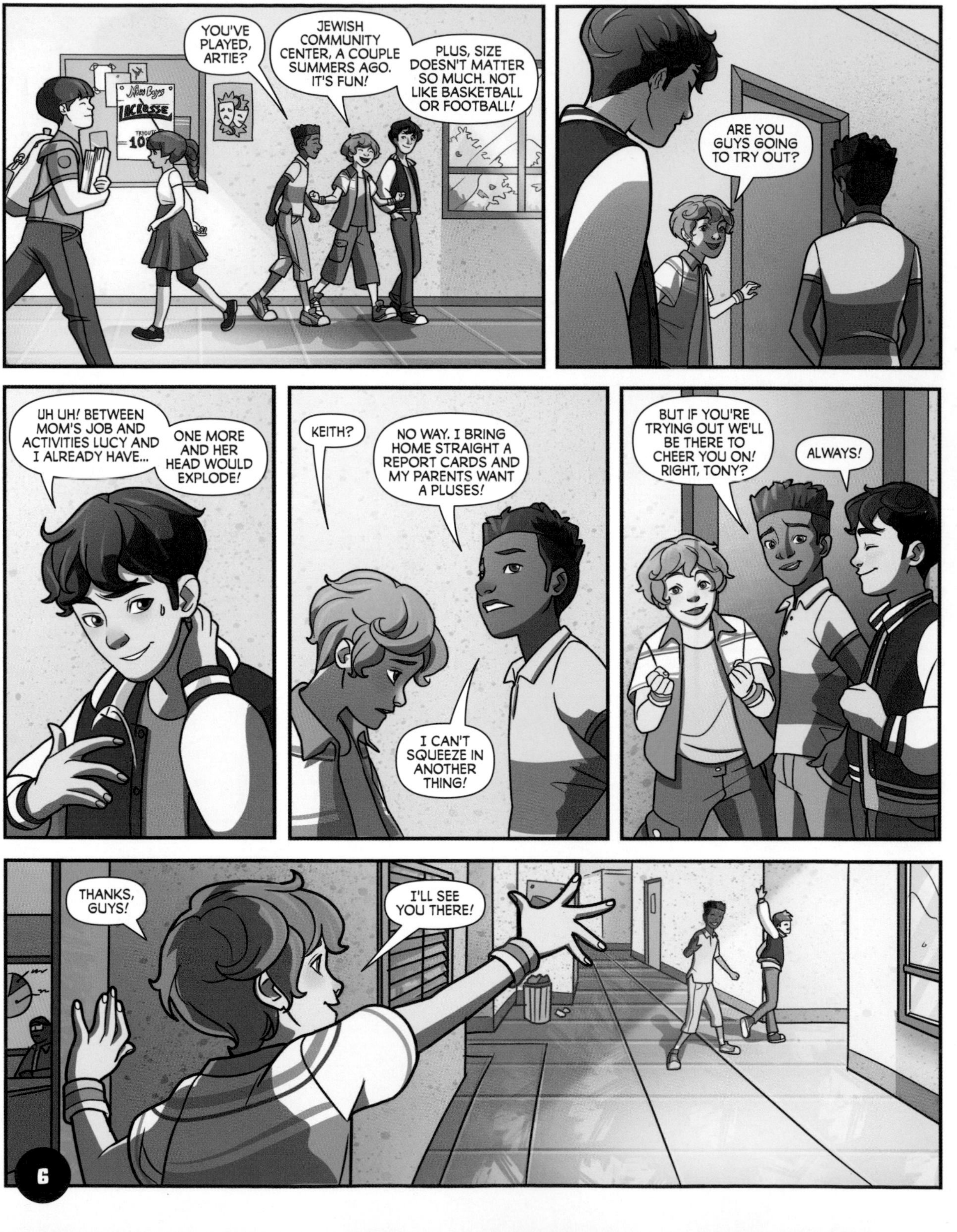
YOU'VE PLAYED, ARTIE?
JEWISH COMMUNITY CENTER, A COUPLE SUMMERS AGO. IT'S FUN!
PLUS, SIZE DOESN'T MATTER SO MUCH. NOT LIKE BASKETBALL OR FOOTBALL!
ARE YOU GUYS GOING TO TRY OUT?
UH UH! BETWEEN MOM'S JOB AND ACTIVITIES LUCY AND I ALREADY HAVE...
ONE MORE AND HER HEAD WOULD EXPLODE!
KEITH?
NO WAY. I BRING HOME STRAIGHT A REPORT CARDS AND MY PARENTS WANT A PLUSES!
I CAN'T SQUEEZE IN ANOTHER THING!
BUT IF YOU'RE TRYING OUT WE'LL BE THERE TO CHEER YOU ON! RIGHT, TONY?
ALWAYS!
THANKS, GUYS!
I'LL SEE YOU THERE!

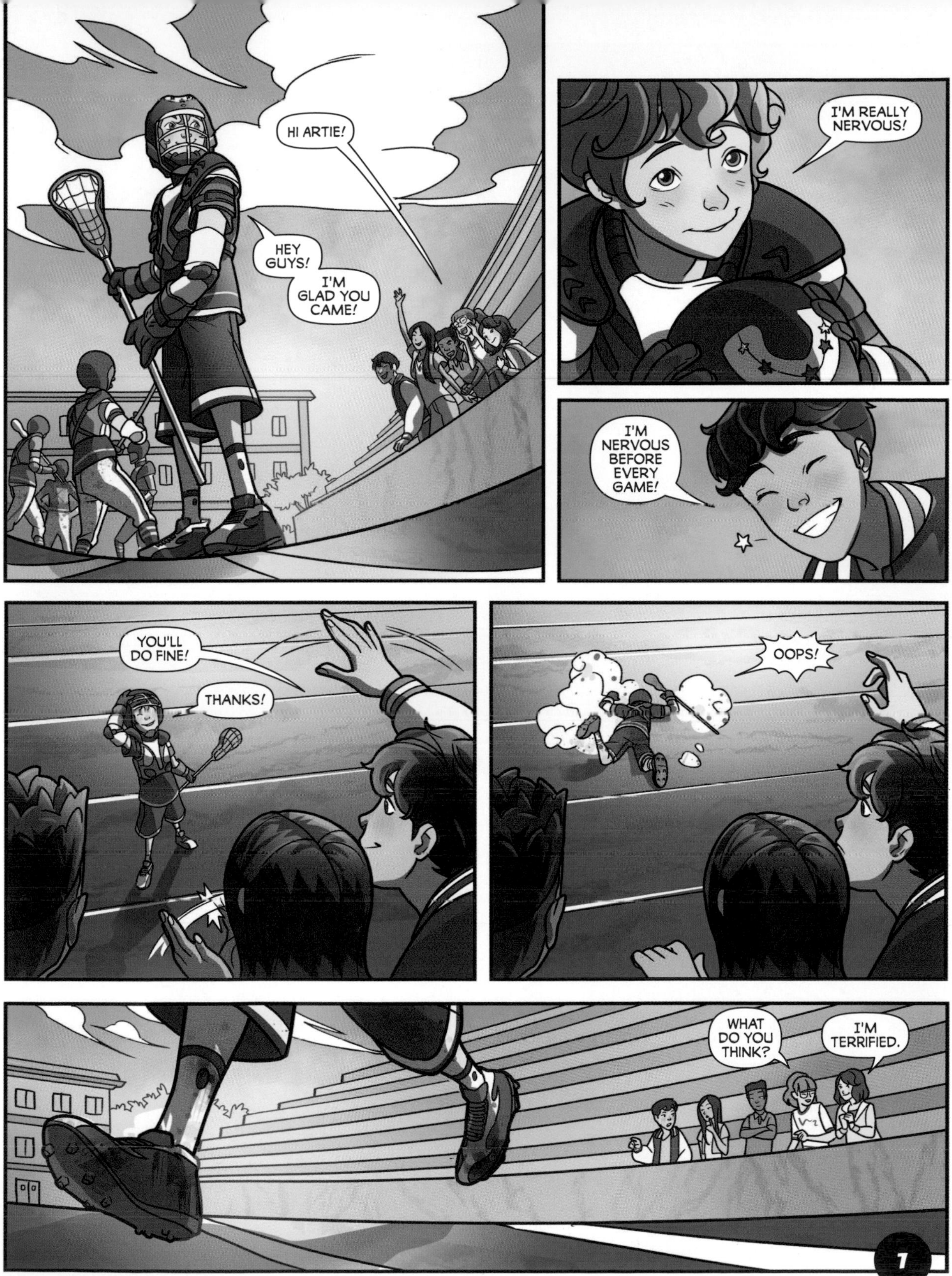
HI ARTIE!
HEY GUYS!
I'M GLAD YOU CAME!
I'M REALLY NERVOUS!
I'M NERVOUS BEFORE EVERY GAME!
YOU'LL DO FINE!
THANKS!
OOPS!
WHAT DO YOU THINK?
I'M TERRIFIED.

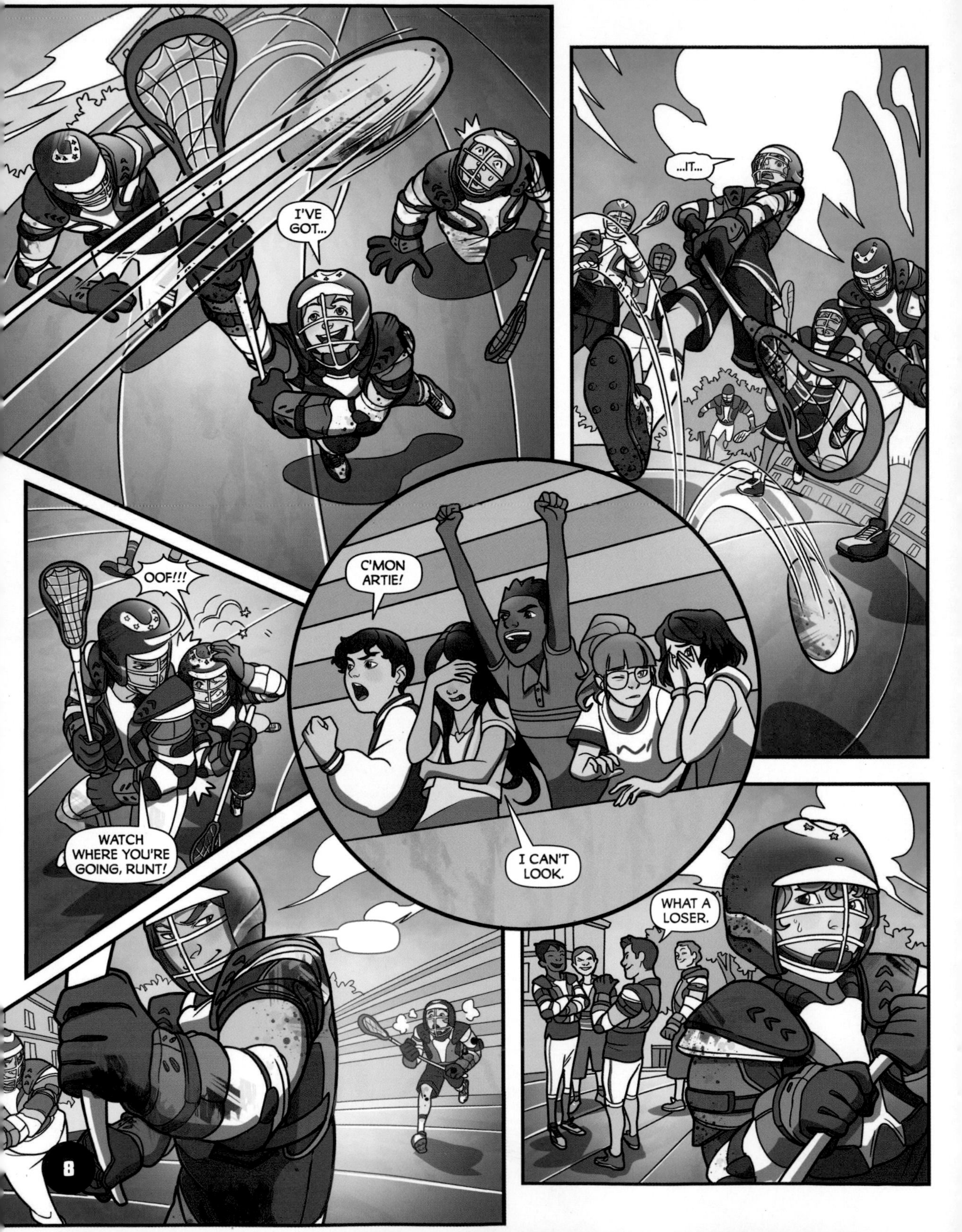

I'VE GOT...
...IT...
C'MON ARTIE!
I CAN'T LOOK.
OOF!!!
WATCH WHERE YOU'RE GOING, RUNT!
WHAT A LOSER.

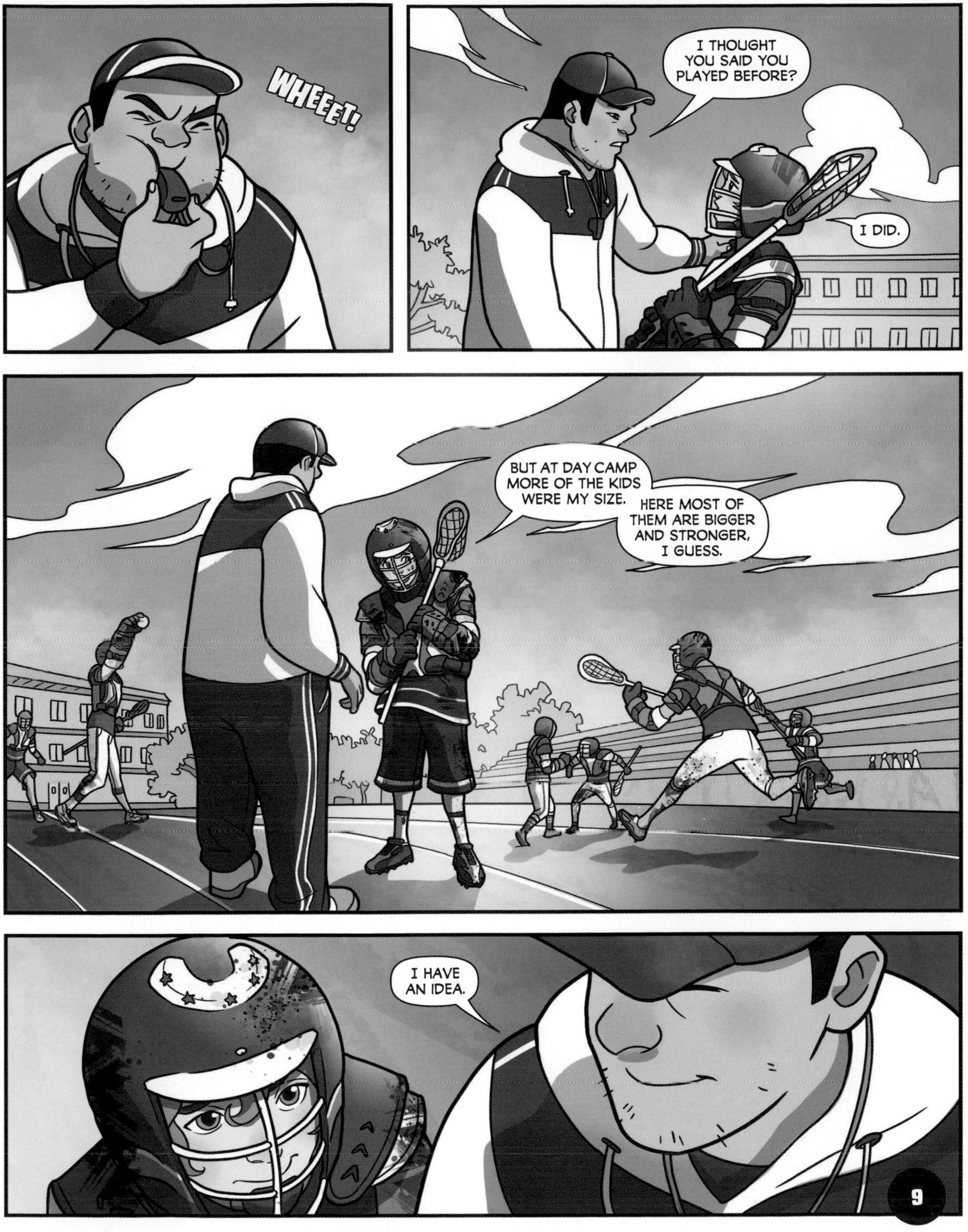
WHEEET!
I THOUGHT YOU SAID YOU PLAYED BEFORE?
I DID.
BUT AT DAY CAMP MORE OF THE KIDS WERE MY SIZE.
HERE MOST OF THEM ARE BIGGER AND STRONGER, I GUESS.
I HAVE AN IDEA.

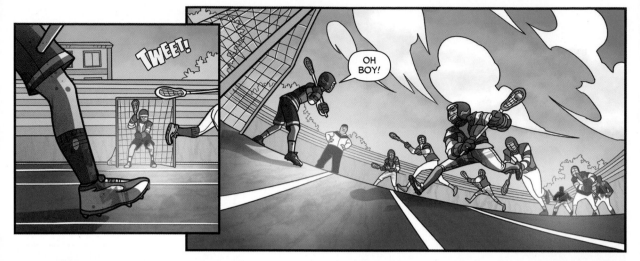

TWEET!

OH BOY!

YIKES!

NOT AGAIN!

WHEW!

UH OH!

KCCCSH

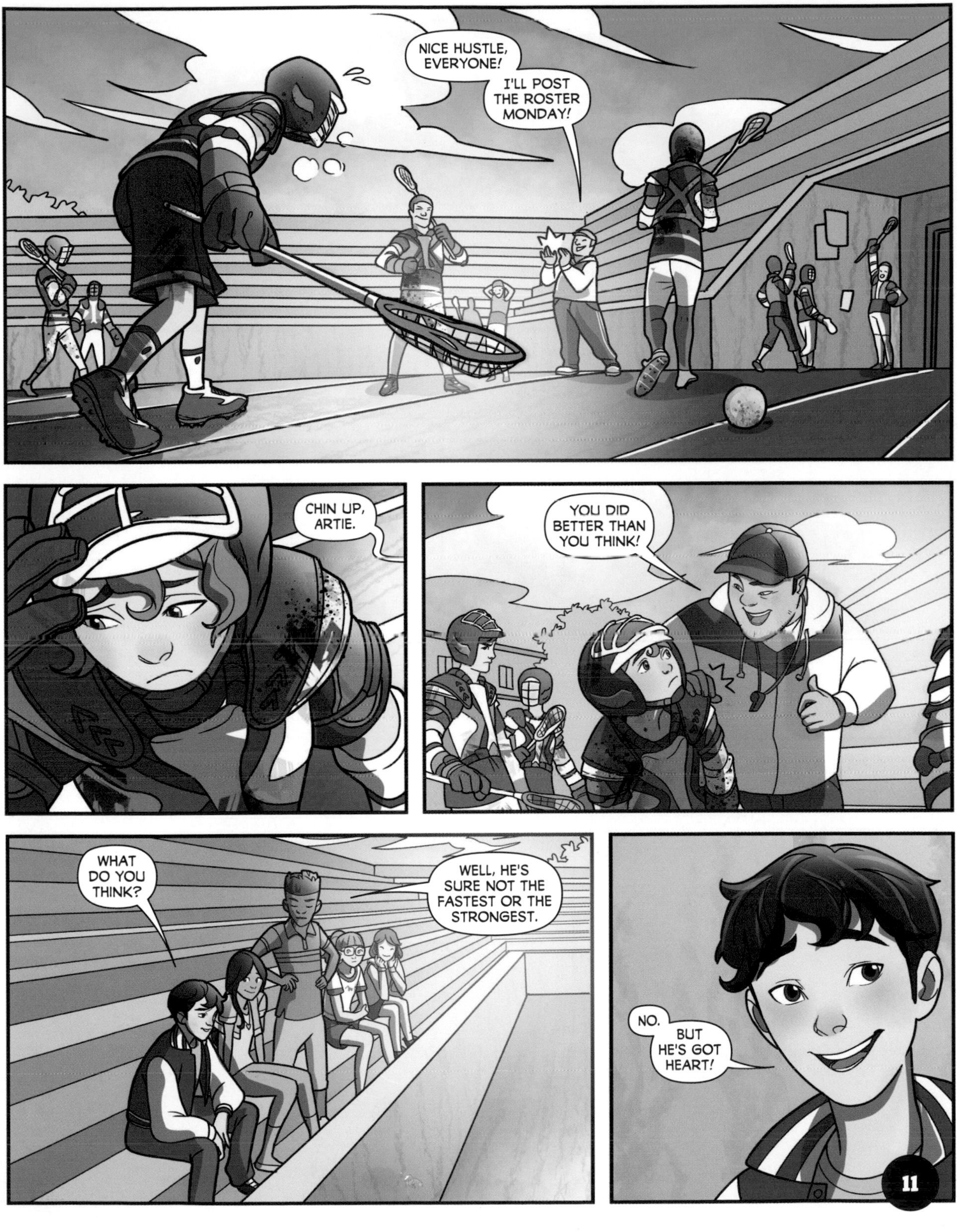
NICE HUSTLE, EVERYONE!
I'LL POST THE ROSTER MONDAY!
CHIN UP, ARTIE.
YOU DID BETTER THAN YOU THINK!
WHAT DO YOU THINK?
WELL, HE'S SURE NOT THE FASTEST OR THE STRONGEST.
NO.
BUT HE'S GOT HEART!

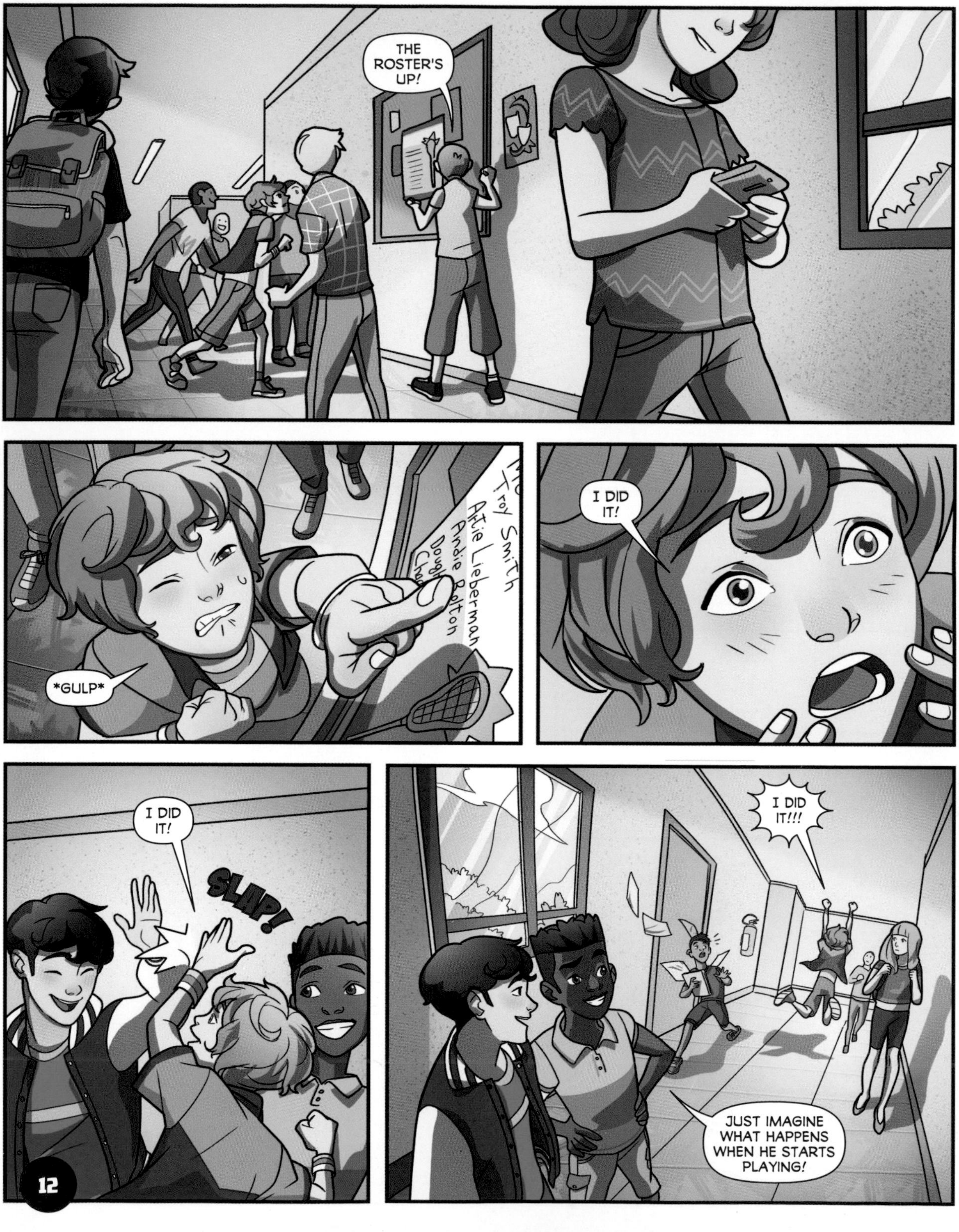
THE ROSTER'S UP!
Troy Smith
Artie Lieberman
Andie Bolton
GULP
I DID IT!
I DID IT!
SLAP!
I DID IT!!!
JUST IMAGINE WHAT HAPPENS WHEN HE STARTS PLAYING!

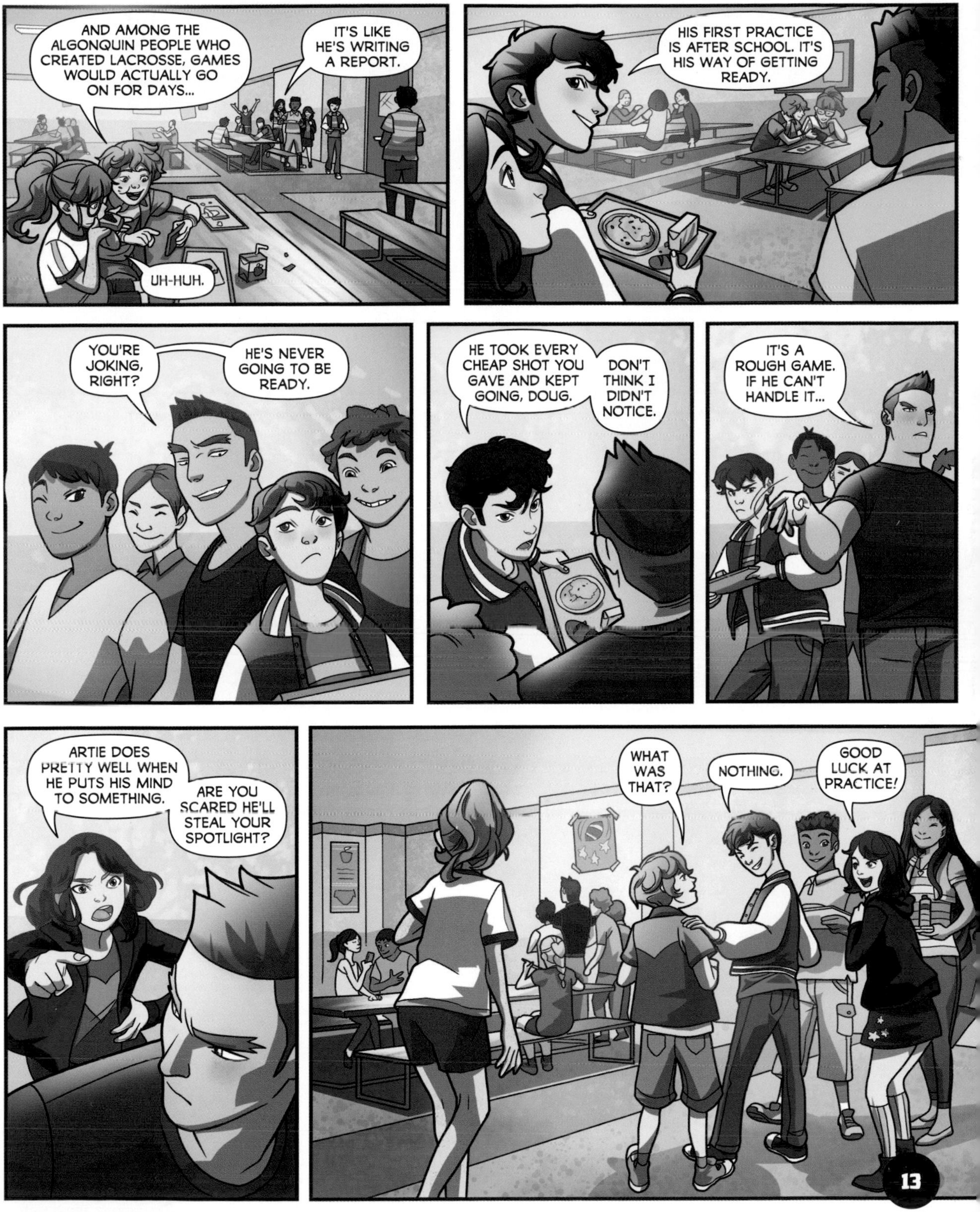
AND AMONG THE ALGONQUIN PEOPLE WHO CREATED LACROSSE, GAMES WOULD ACTUALLY GO ON FOR DAYS...
IT'S LIKE HE'S WRITING A REPORT.
UH-HUH.
HIS FIRST PRACTICE IS AFTER SCHOOL. IT'S HIS WAY OF GETTING READY.
YOU'RE JOKING, RIGHT?
HE'S NEVER GOING TO BE READY.
HE TOOK EVERY CHEAP SHOT YOU GAVE AND KEPT GOING, DOUG.
DON'T THINK I DIDN'T NOTICE.
IT'S A ROUGH GAME. IF HE CAN'T HANDLE IT...
ARTIE DOES PRETTY WELL WHEN HE PUTS HIS MIND TO SOMETHING.
ARE YOU SCARED HE'LL STEAL YOUR SPOTLIGHT?
WHAT WAS THAT?
NOTHING.
GOOD LUCK AT PRACTICE!

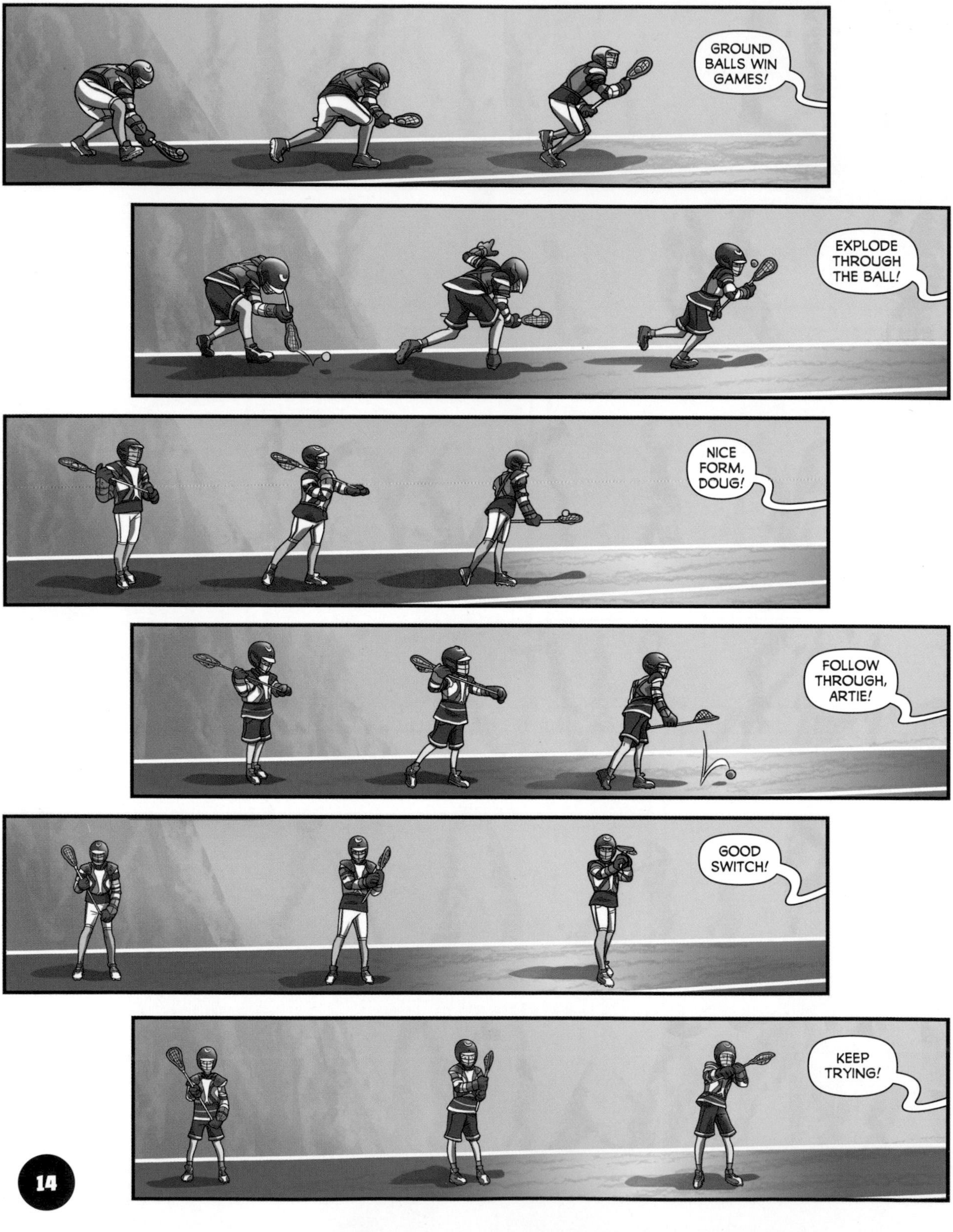
GROUND BALLS WIN GAMES!
EXPLODE THROUGH THE BALL!
NICE FORM, DOUG!
FOLLOW THROUGH, ARTIE!
GOOD SWITCH!
KEEP TRYING!

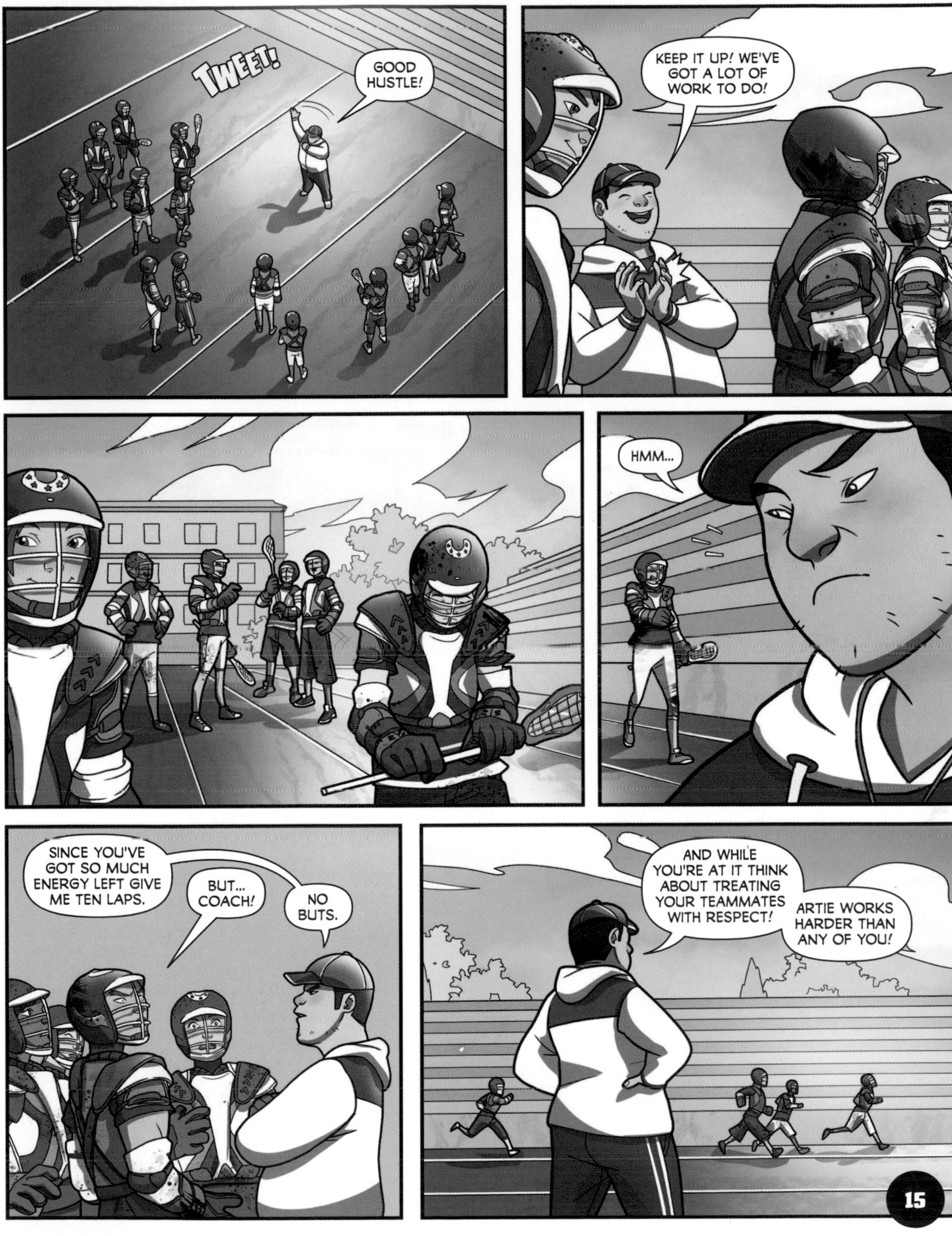
TWEET!
GOOD HUSTLE!
KEEP IT UP! WE'VE GOT A LOT OF WORK TO DO!
HMM...
SINCE YOU'VE GOT SO MUCH ENERGY LEFT GIVE ME TEN LAPS.
BUT... COACH!
NO BUTS.
AND WHILE YOU'RE AT IT THINK ABOUT TREATING YOUR TEAMMATES WITH RESPECT!
ARTIE WORKS HARDER THAN ANY OF YOU!

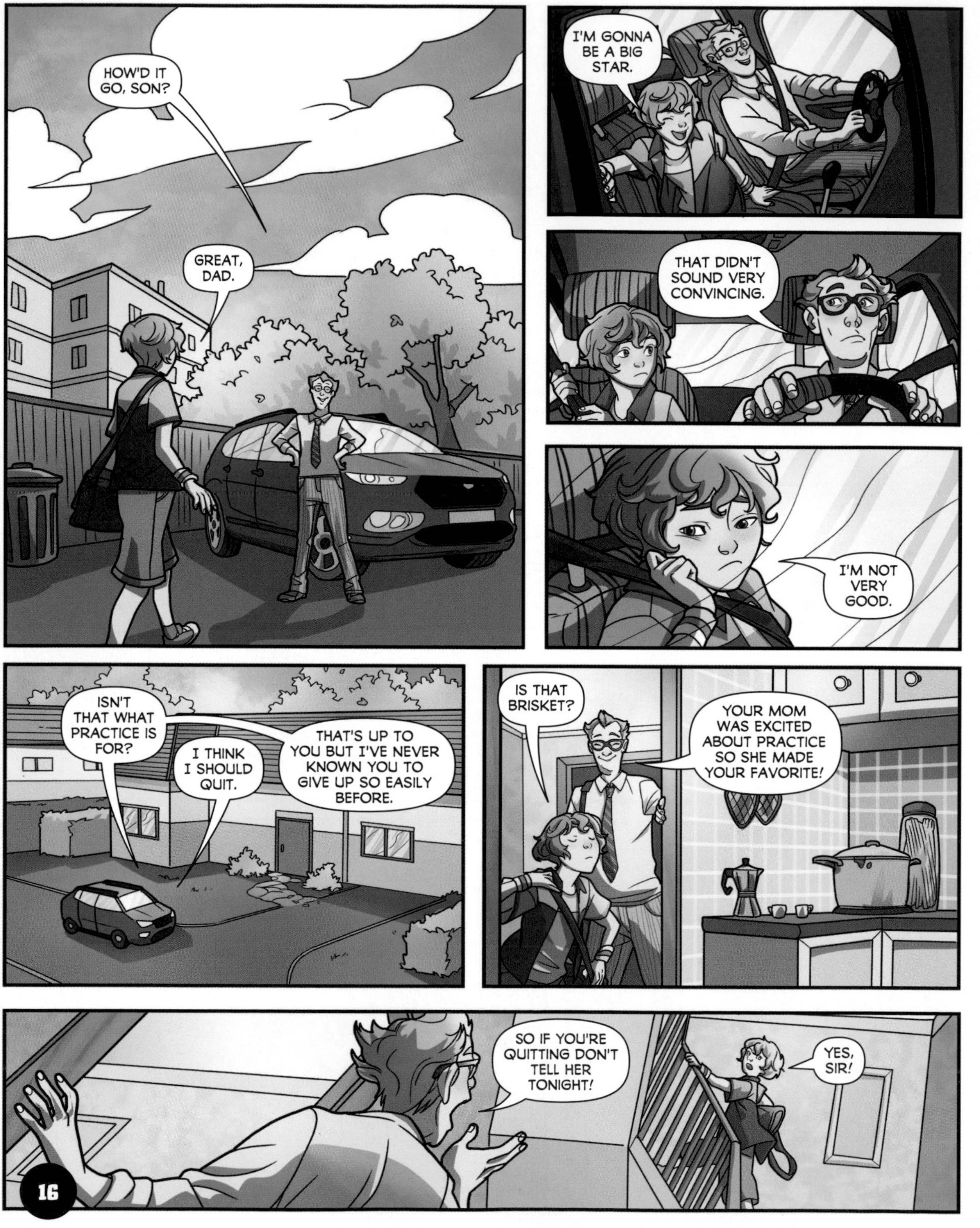
HOW'D IT GO, SON?
GREAT, DAD.
I'M GONNA BE A BIG STAR.
THAT DIDN'T SOUND VERY CONVINCING.
I'M NOT VERY GOOD.
ISN'T THAT WHAT PRACTICE IS FOR?
I THINK I SHOULD QUIT.
THAT'S UP TO YOU BUT I'VE NEVER KNOWN YOU TO GIVE UP SO EASILY BEFORE.
IS THAT BRISKET?
YOUR MOM WAS EXCITED ABOUT PRACTICE SO SHE MADE YOUR FAVORITE!
SO IF YOU'RE QUITTING DON'T TELL HER TONIGHT!
YES, SIR!

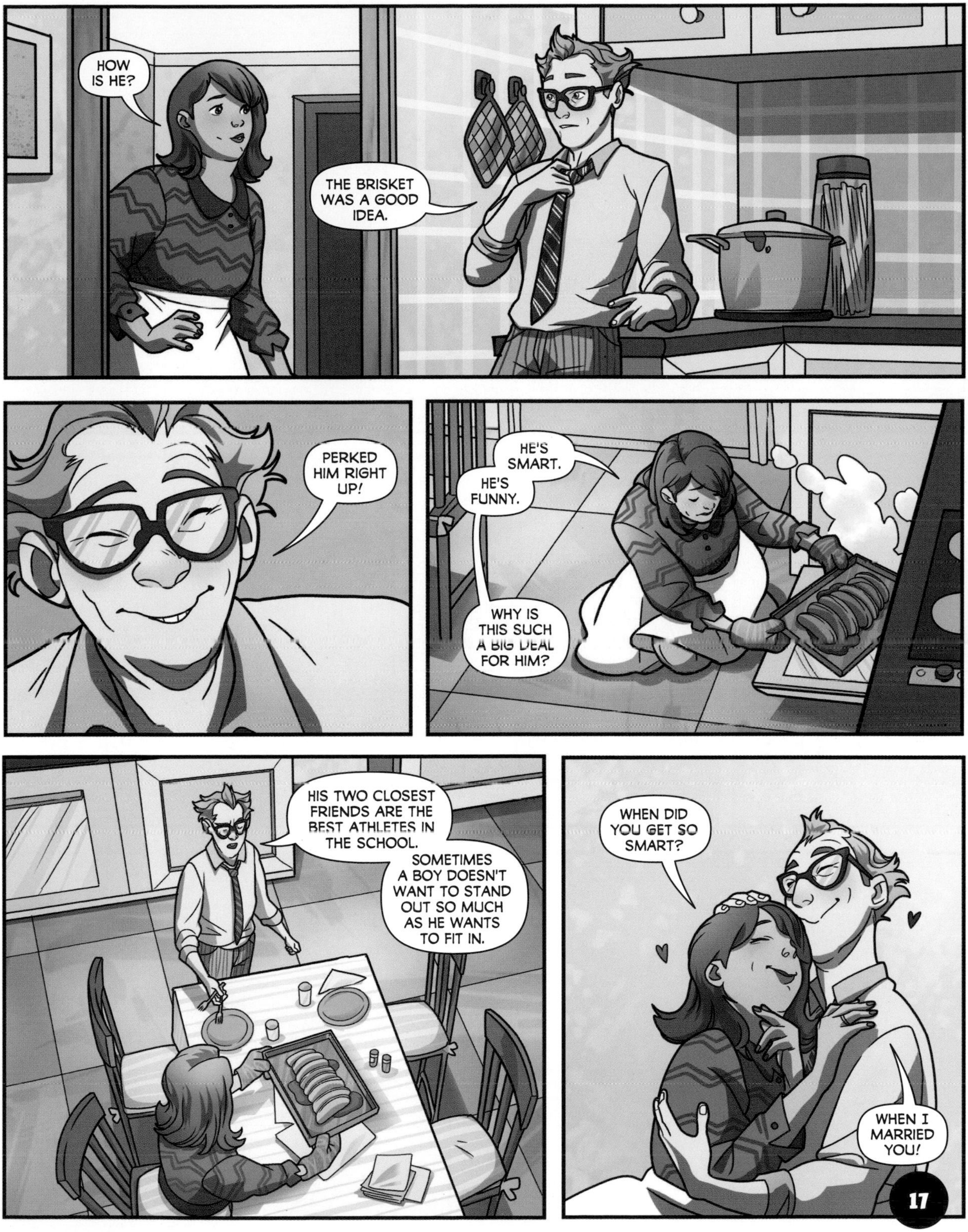
HOW IS HE?
THE BRISKET WAS A GOOD IDEA.
PERKED HIM RIGHT UP!
HE'S SMART.
HE'S FUNNY.
WHY IS THIS SUCH A BIG DEAL FOR HIM?
HIS TWO CLOSEST FRIENDS ARE THE BEST ATHLETES IN THE SCHOOL.
SOMETIMES A BOY DOESN'T WANT TO STAND OUT SO MUCH AS HE WANTS TO FIT IN.
WHEN DID YOU GET SO SMART?
WHEN I MARRIED YOU!

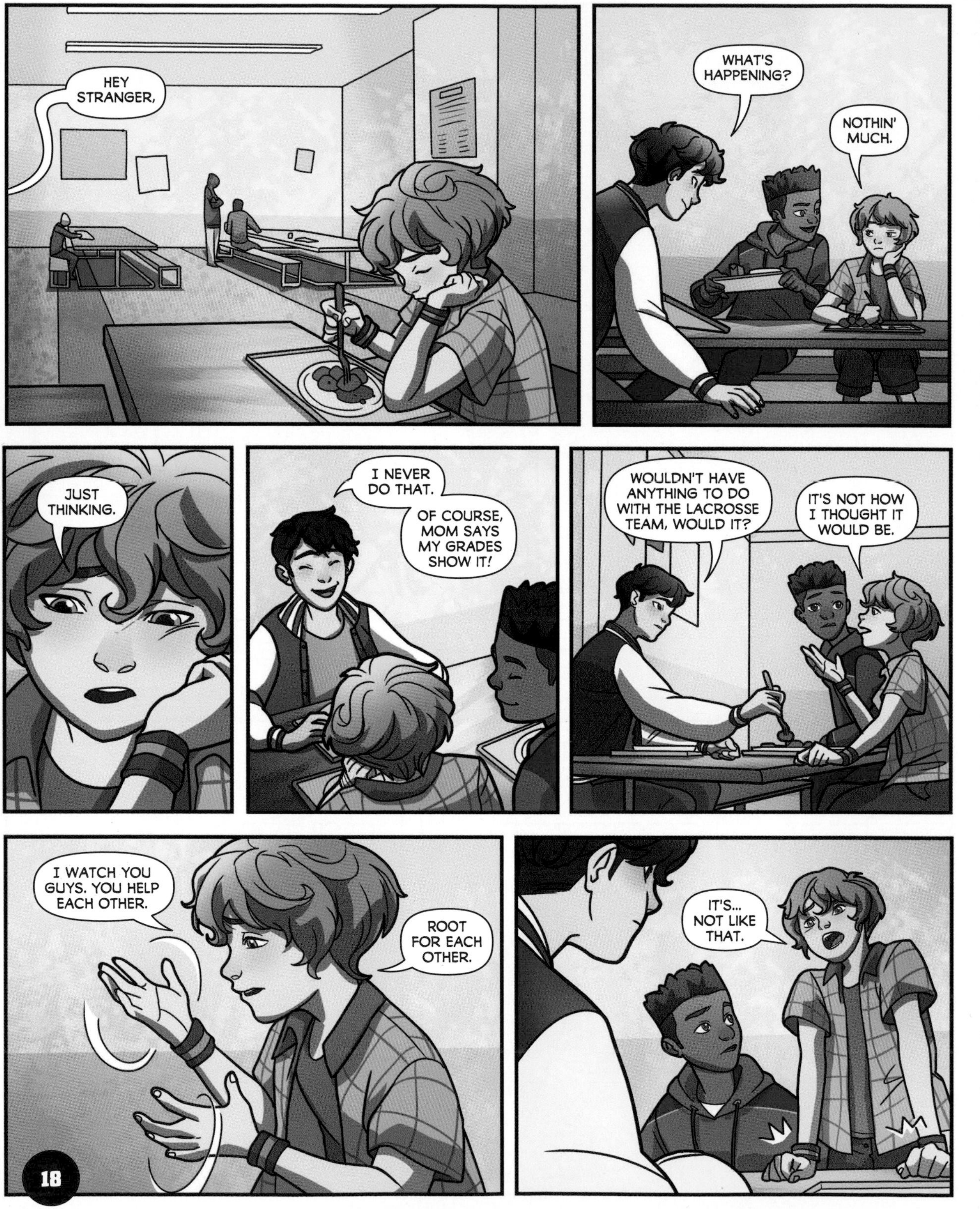

HEY STRANGER,
WHAT'S HAPPENING?
NOTHIN' MUCH.
JUST THINKING.
I NEVER DO THAT.
OF COURSE, MOM SAYS MY GRADES SHOW IT!
WOULDN'T HAVE ANYTHING TO DO WITH THE LACROSSE TEAM, WOULD IT?
IT'S NOT HOW I THOUGHT IT WOULD BE.
I WATCH YOU GUYS. YOU HELP EACH OTHER.
ROOT FOR EACH OTHER.
IT'S... NOT LIKE THAT.

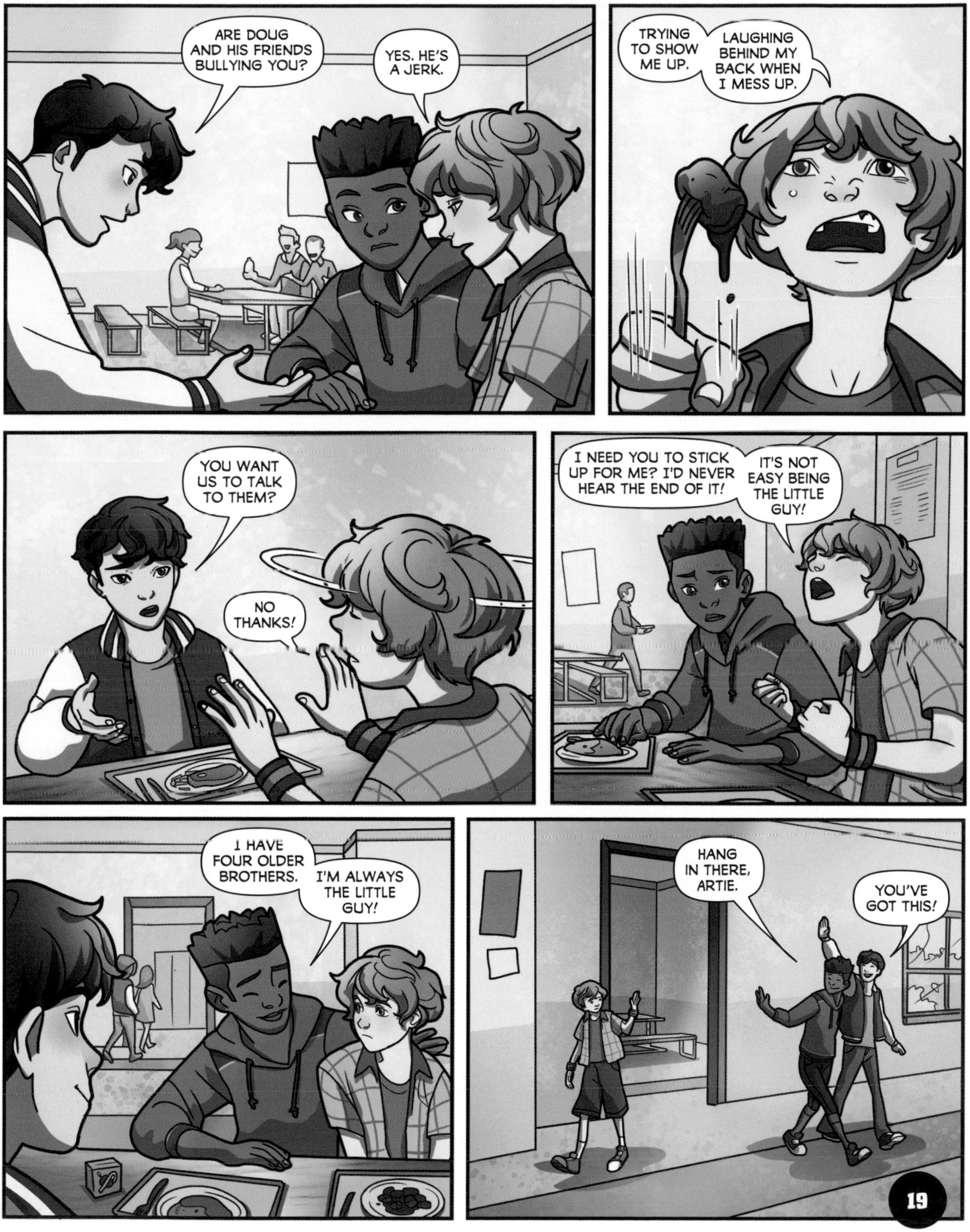
ARE DOUG AND HIS FRIENDS BULLYING YOU?
YES. HE'S A JERK.
TRYING TO SHOW ME UP.
LAUGHING BEHIND MY BACK WHEN I MESS UP.
YOU WANT US TO TALK TO THEM?
NO THANKS!
I NEED YOU TO STICK UP FOR ME? I'D NEVER HEAR THE END OF IT!
IT'S NOT EASY BEING THE LITTLE GUY!
I HAVE FOUR OLDER BROTHERS.
I'M ALWAYS THE LITTLE GUY!
HANG IN THERE, ARTIE.
YOU'VE GOT THIS!

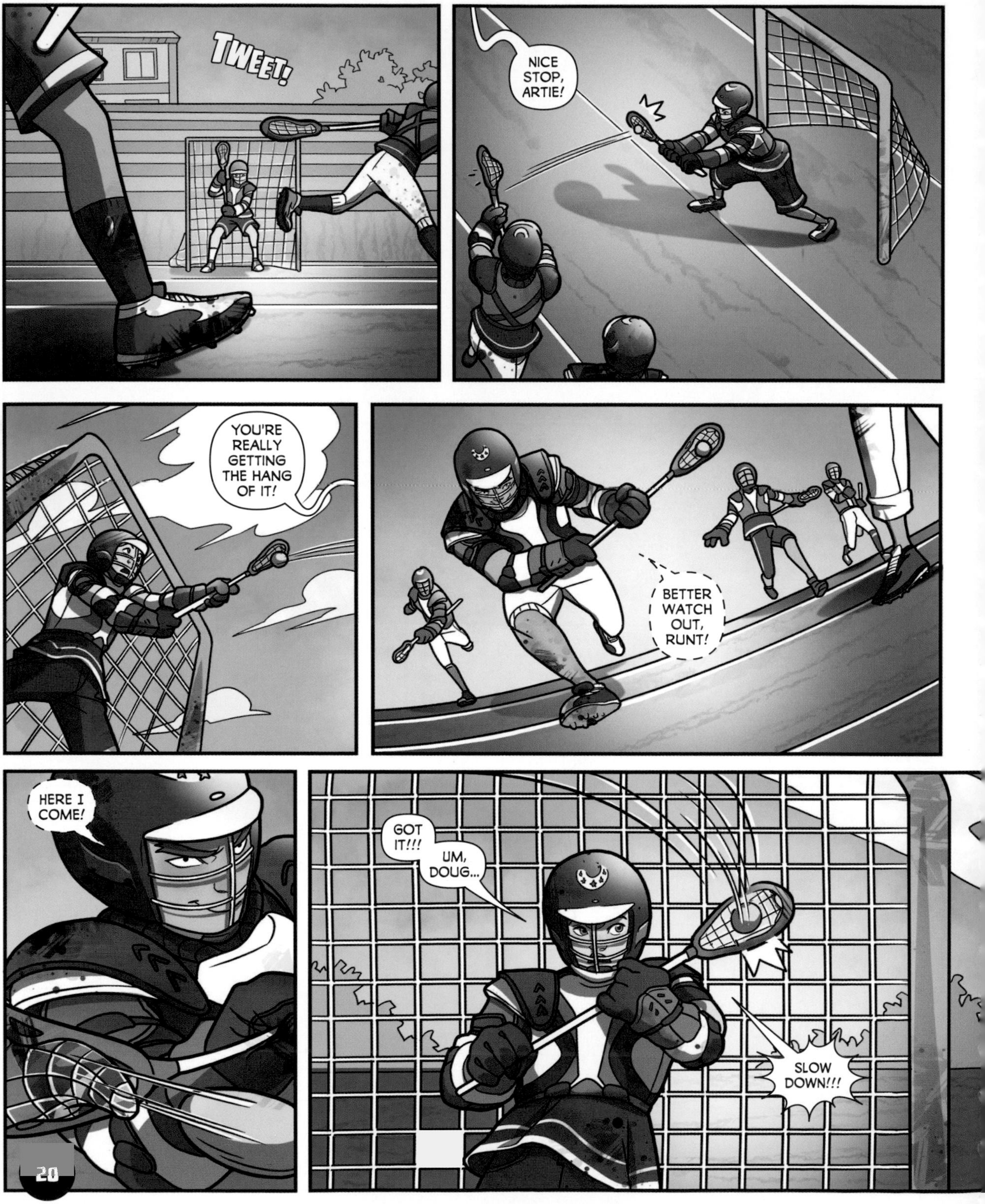
TWEET!
NICE STOP, ARTIE!
YOU'RE REALLY GETTING THE HANG OF IT!
BETTER WATCH OUT, RUNT!
HERE I COME!
GOT IT!!!
UM, DOUG...
SLOW DOWN!!!

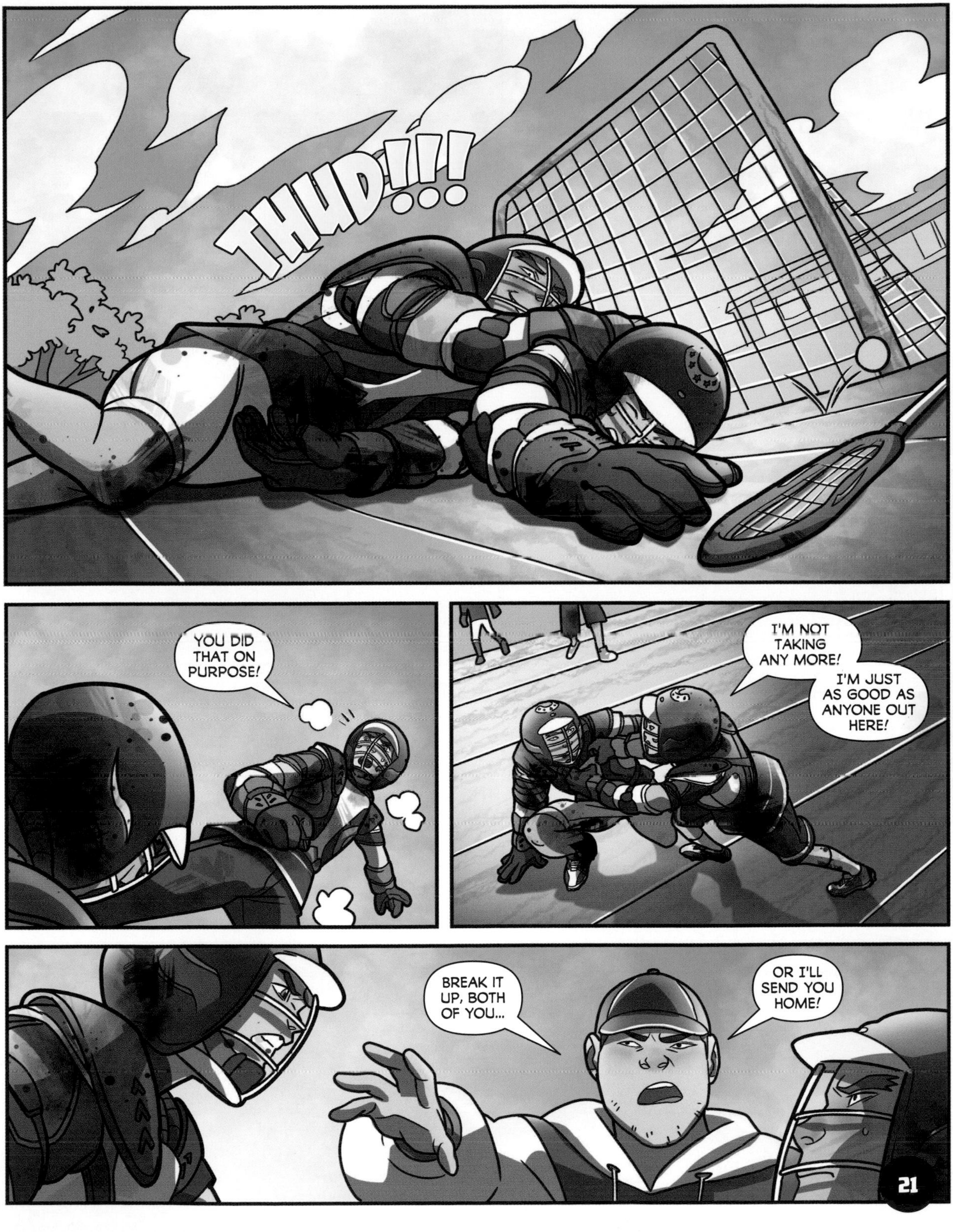
THUD!!!
YOU DID THAT ON PURPOSE!
I'M NOT TAKING ANY MORE!
I'M JUST AS GOOD AS ANYONE OUT HERE!
BREAK IT UP, BOTH OF YOU...
OR I'LL SEND YOU HOME!

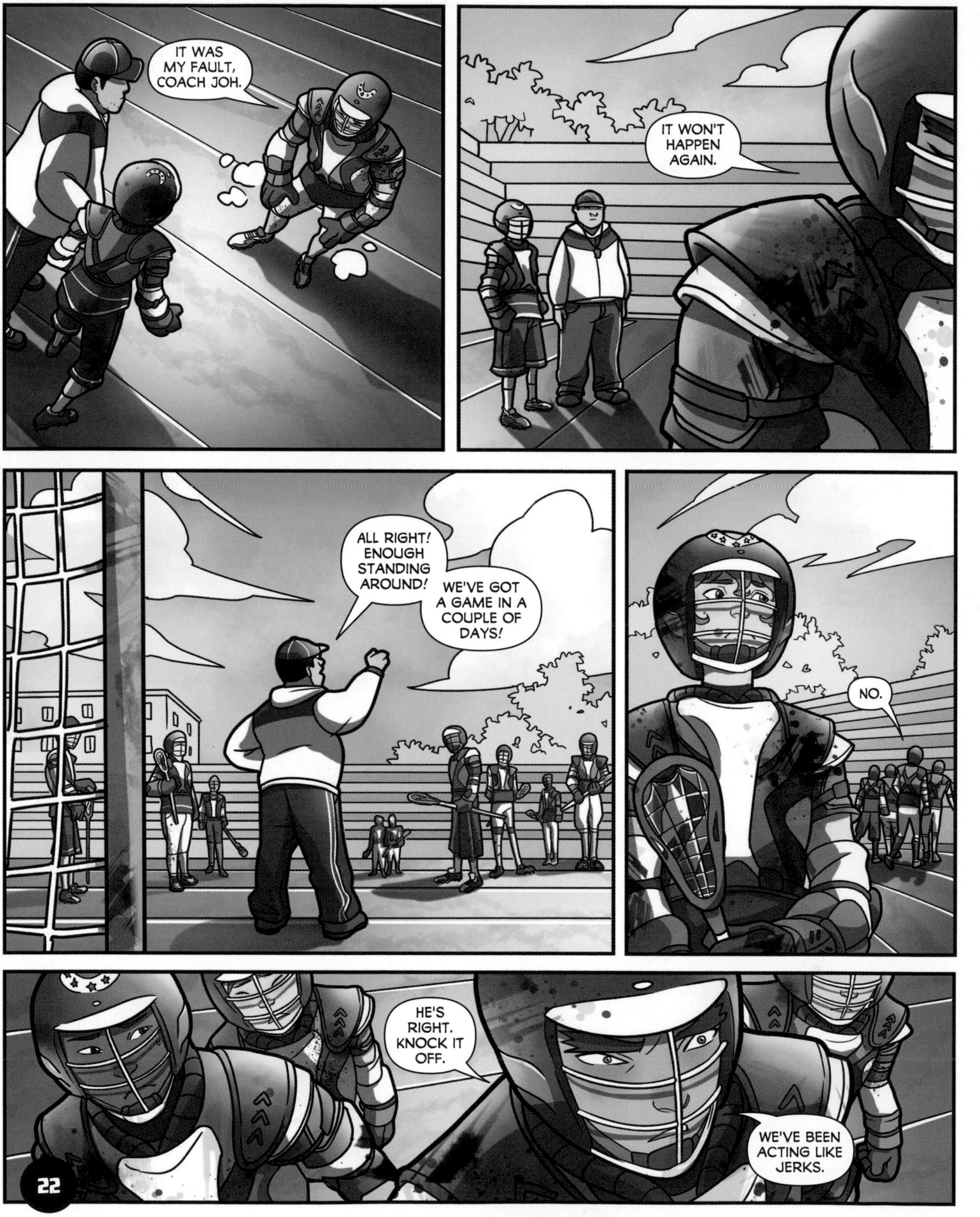
IT WAS MY FAULT, COACH JOH.
IT WON'T HAPPEN AGAIN.
ALL RIGHT! ENOUGH STANDING AROUND!
WE'VE GOT A GAME IN A COUPLE OF DAYS!
NO.
HE'S RIGHT. KNOCK IT OFF.
WE'VE BEEN ACTING LIKE JERKS.

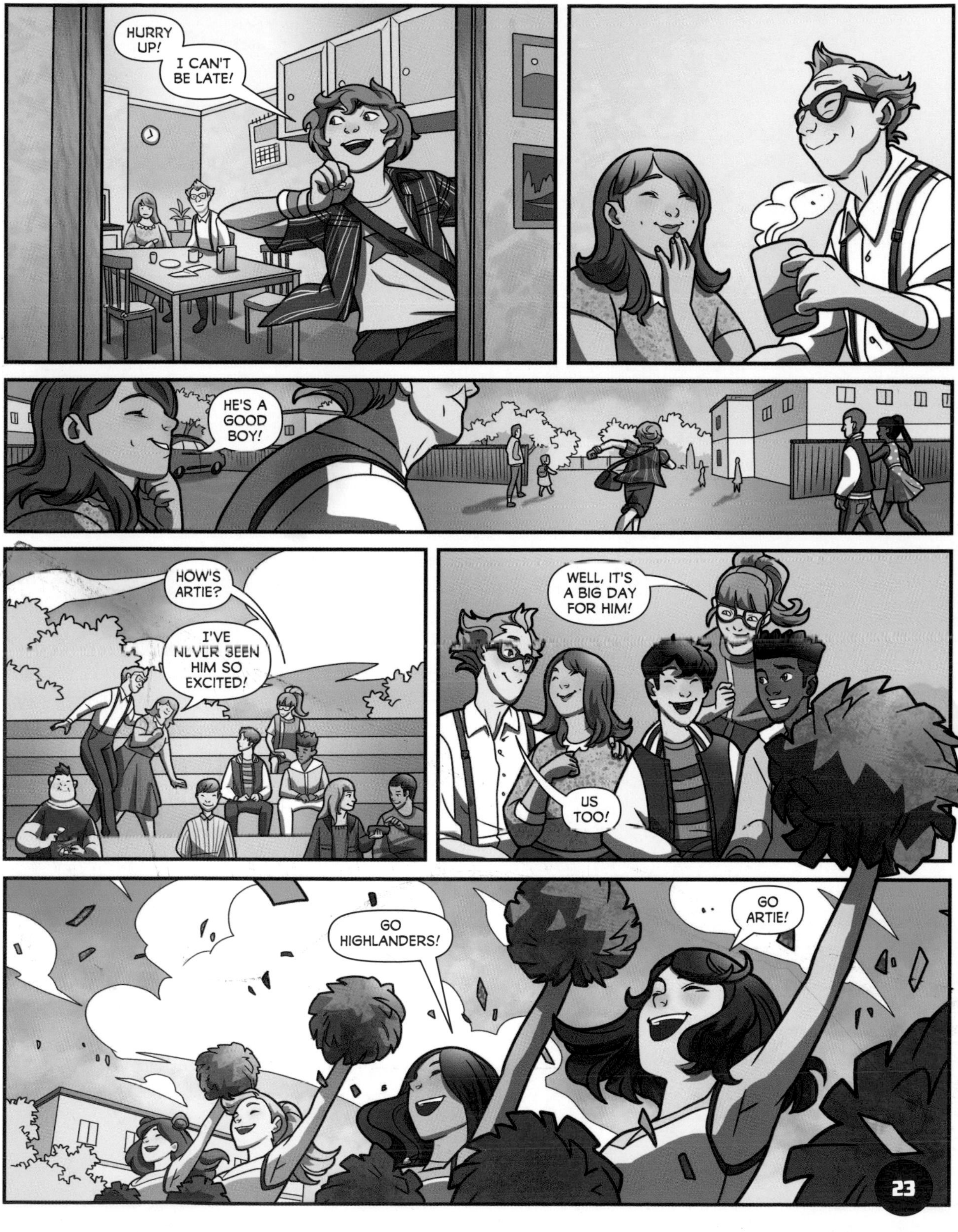
HURRY UP!
I CAN'T BE LATE!
HE'S A GOOD BOY!
HOW'S ARTIE?
I'VE NEVER SEEN HIM SO EXCITED!
WELL, IT'S A BIG DAY FOR HIM!
US TOO!
GO HIGHLANDERS!
GO ARTIE!

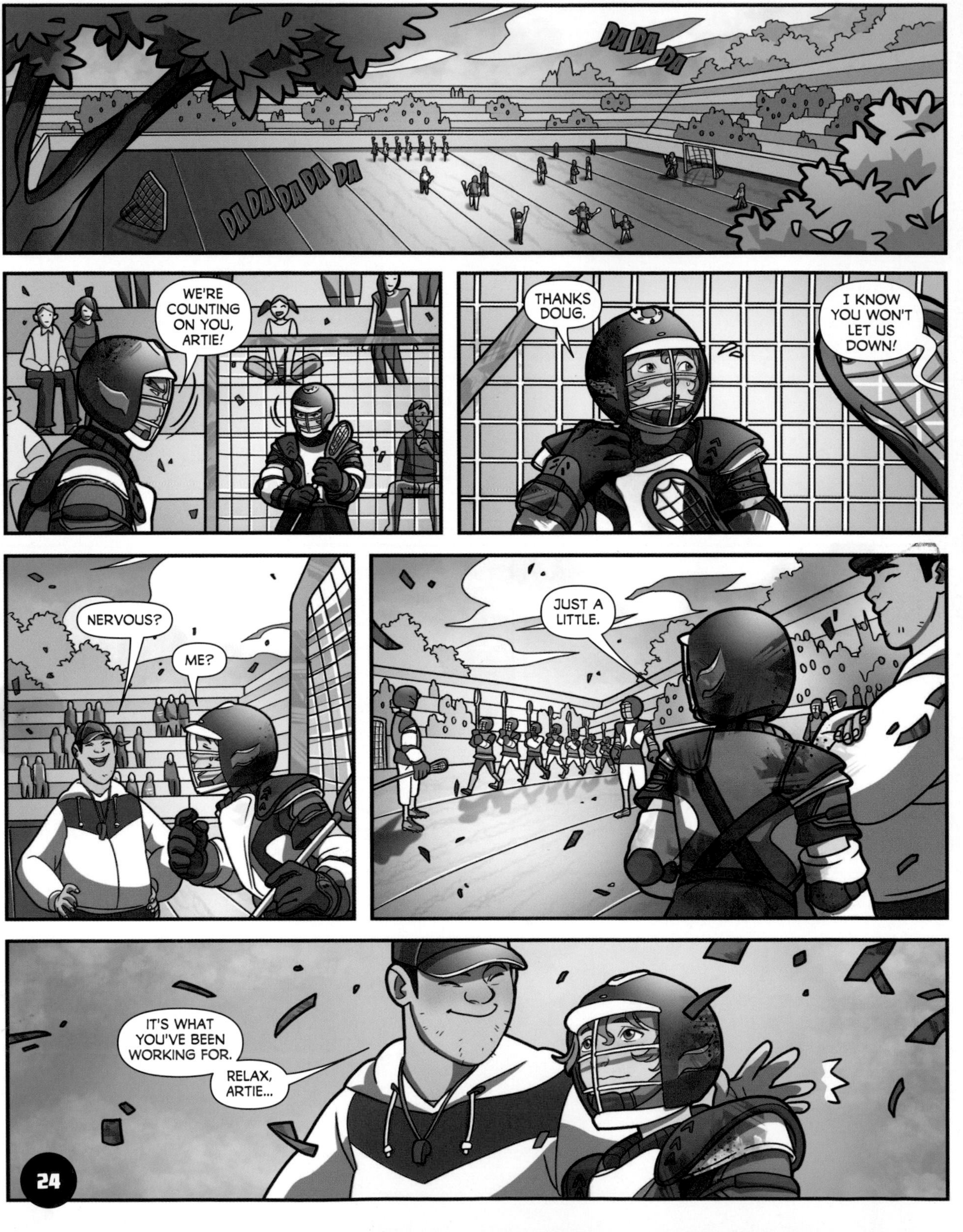
DA DA DA DA DA
DA DA DA
WE'RE COUNTING ON YOU, ARTIE!
THANKS DOUG.
I KNOW YOU WON'T LET US DOWN!
NERVOUS?
ME?
JUST A LITTLE.
RELAX, ARTIE...
IT'S WHAT YOU'VE BEEN WORKING FOR.

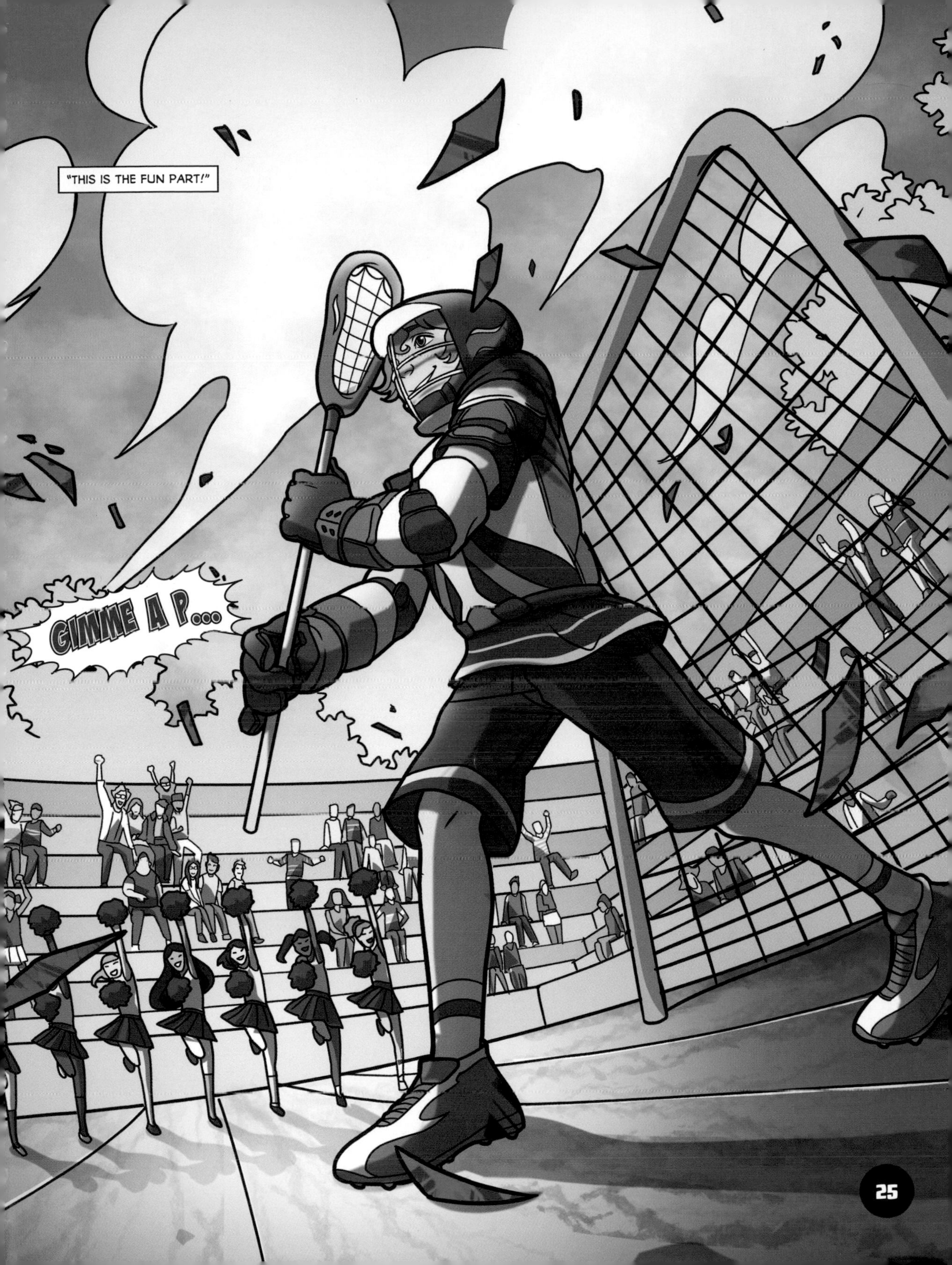
"THIS IS THE FUN PART!"
GIMME A P...

ARTIE &

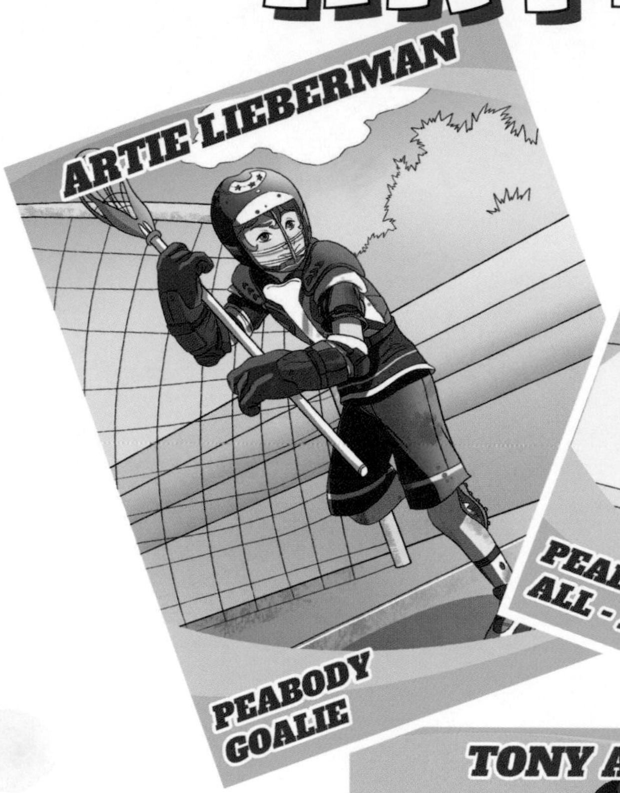
ARTIE LIEBERMAN
PEABODY GOALIE

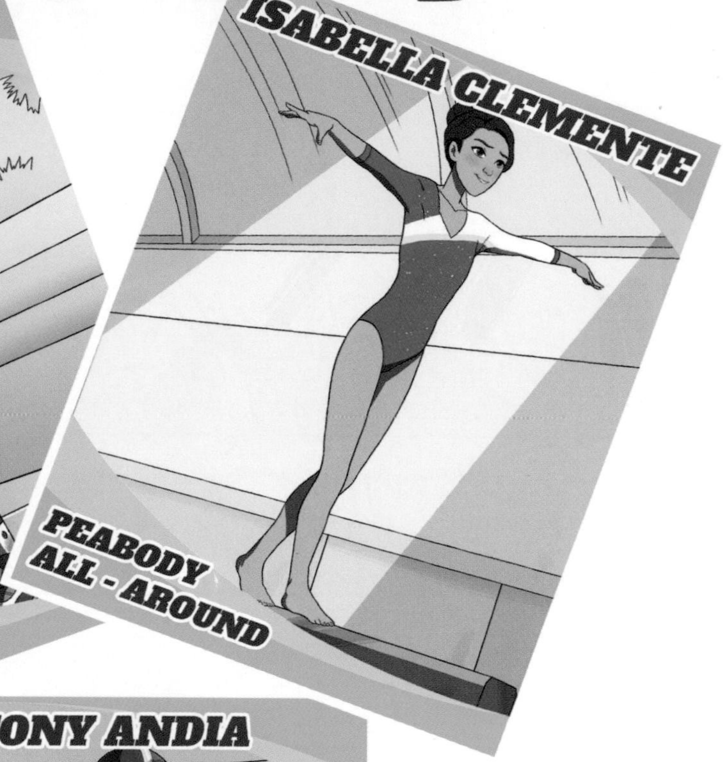
ISABELLA CLEMENTE
PEABODY ALL - AROUND

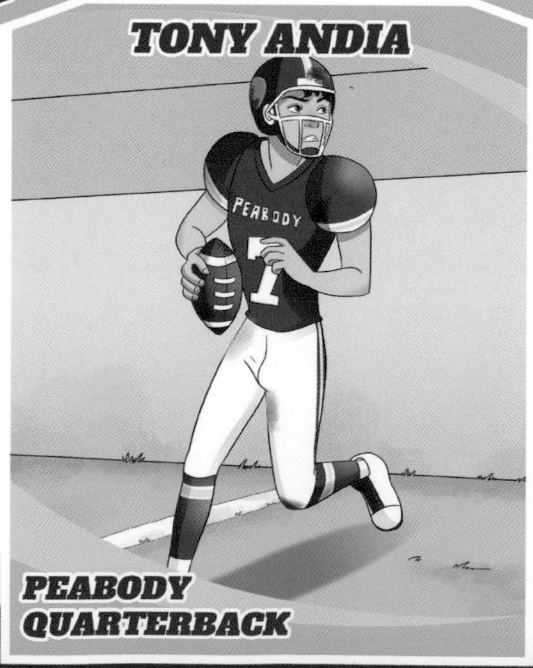
TONY ANDIA
PEABODY
1
PEABODY QUARTERBACK

FRIENDS

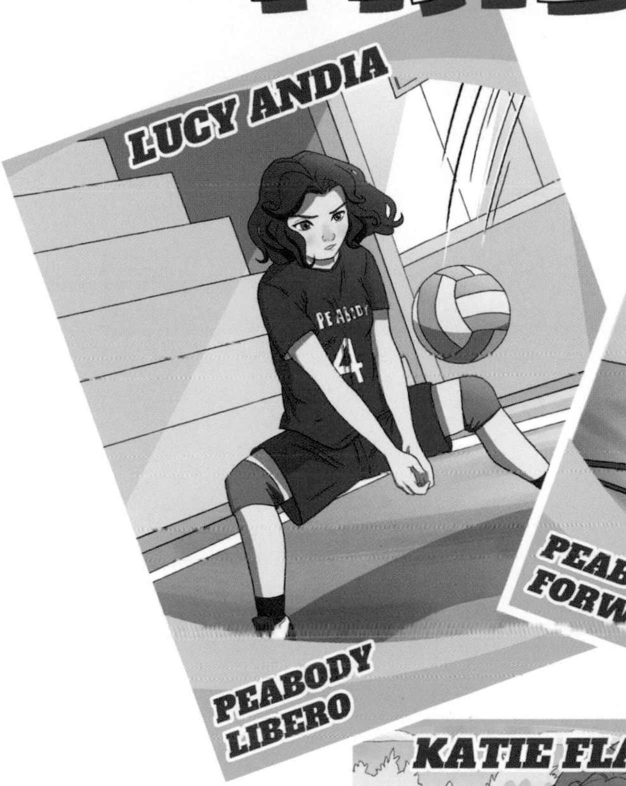
LUCY ANDIA
PEABODY
4
PEABODY
LIBERO

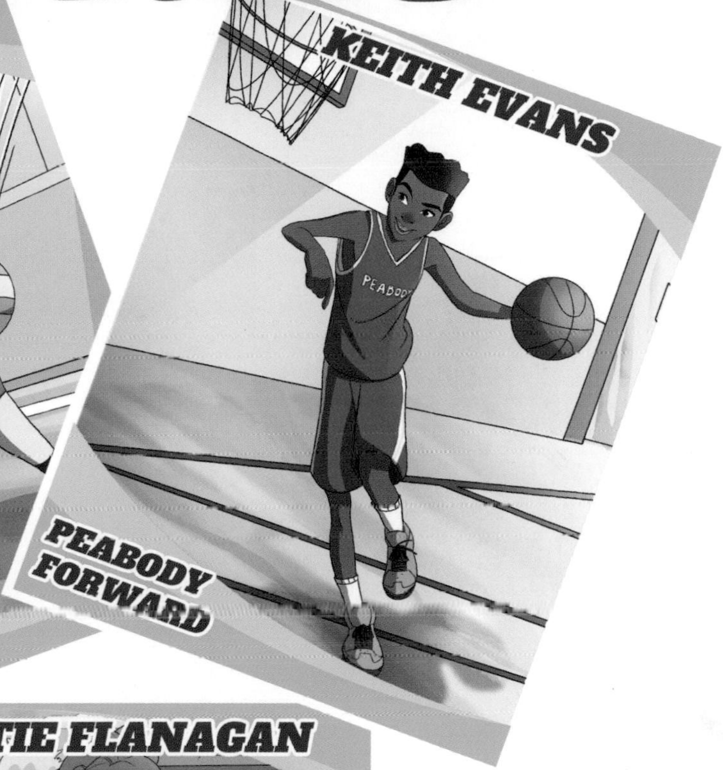
KEITH EVANS
PEABODY
PEABODY
FORWARD

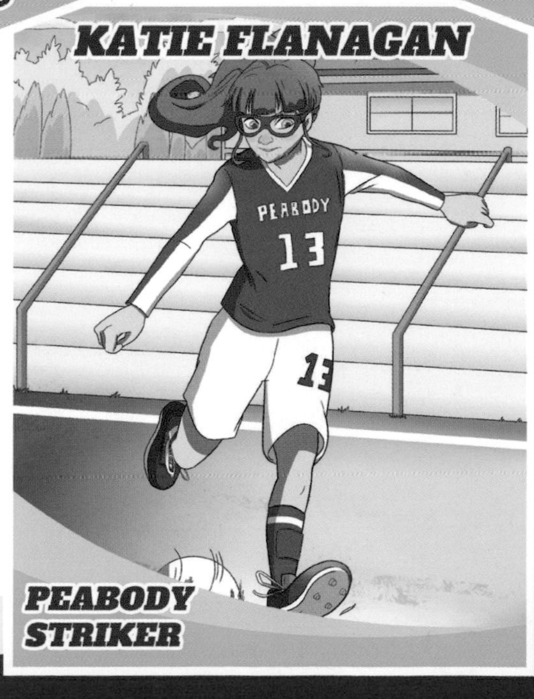
KATIE FLANAGAN
PEABODY
13
13
PEABODY
STRIKER

LACROSSE

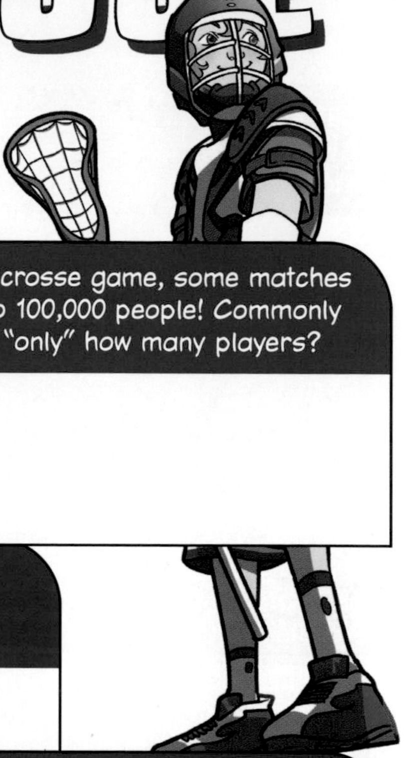

1. Lacrosse is the national summer sport for which country?

a. England
b. United States
c. Canada
d. Australia

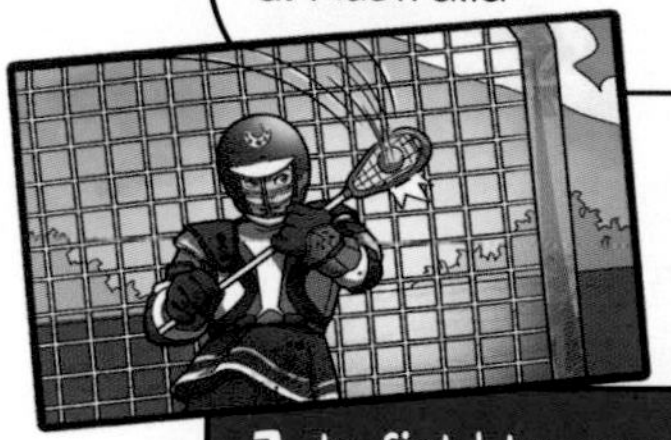

2. In the original lacrosse game, some matches could involve 100 to 100,000 people! Commonly though, it included "only" how many players?

a. 20
b. 200
c. 2000
d. 20,000

3. In field lacrosse, there are 10 players on the field for men's matches. How many are on the field for women's matches?

a. 8
b. 10
c. 12
d. 15

4. Box lacrosse was developed by owners of hockey rinks so lacrosse could be played indoors during the winter. In which decade did this start?

a. 1930s
b. 1950s
c. 1980s
d. 2000s

5. In North American indoor professional lacrosse, the Philadelphia Wings and Toronto Rock have tied the record for the most championships. How many titles has each team won?

a. 3
b. 4
c. 5
d. 6

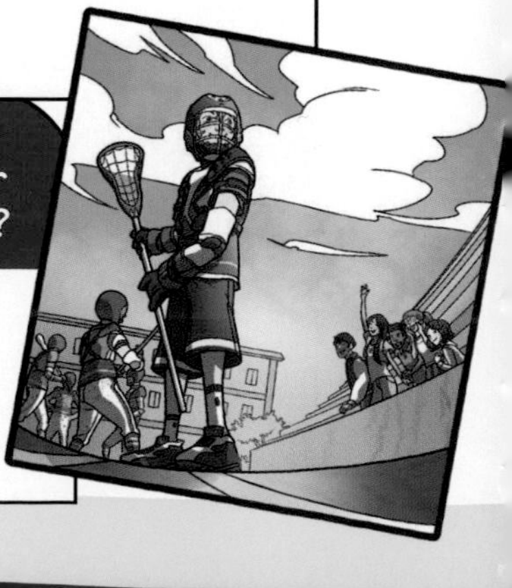

QUIZ

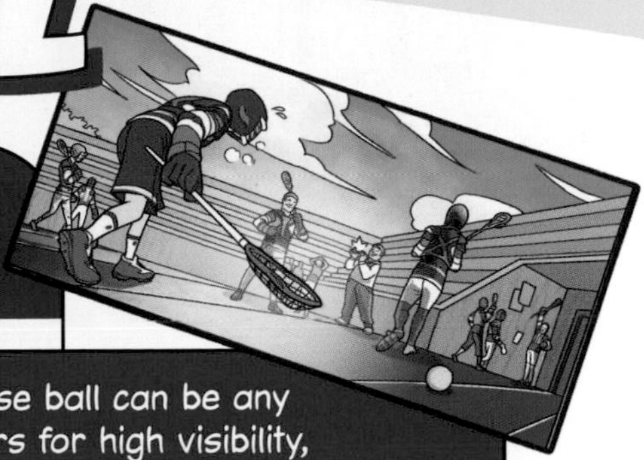

6. The lacrosse ball was originally made of wood, and later of deerskin. Today it is made of what?

a. rock
b. yarn
c. rubber
d. plastic

7. The lacrosse ball can be any of these colors for high visibility, except for:

a. yellow
b. green
c. orange
d. white

8. Lacrosse sticks are usually made of any of these materials except:

a. leather
b. aluminium
c. plastic
d. wood

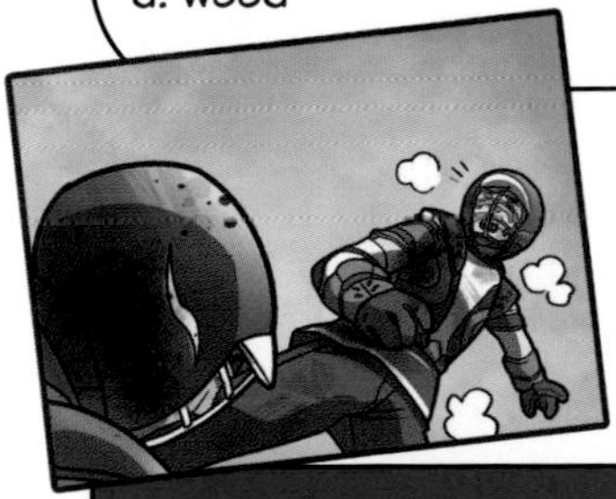

9. The World Lacrosse Championship started in 1967 with 4 teams. How many played in the 2014 tournament?

a. 16
b. 21
c. 29
d. 38

10. How many times has the men's team from the United States won the World Lacrosse Championship since 1967?

a. 2
b. 5
c. 9
d. 12

* Answers on page 32

WHAT DO YOU THINK?

Bullying is when you intimidate, harass, assault, or isolate someone physically or emotionally. It is not okay, and standing up for yourself is the first step. If you need help, talk to friends, parents, or teachers. Don't be a bystander. Show support to someone who is being bullied.

- Why did Artie consider quitting a sport he enjoyed? Have you ever been discouraged and wanted to quit something? What did you do?

- Artie's father did not take a position on whether Artie should quit or not. Why do you think he did this?

- Do you think Doug and his friends would have stopped bullying Artie if Keith and Tony had talked to them? Why or why not?

- Why do you think Coach Joh threatened to kick both players off the team, even though he likely knew Doug was picking on Artie?

- While violence is not a good solution, why do you think Artie standing up for himself helped to stop the tension between him and Doug? What other positive results did this achieve? How would you have handled the situation?

LACROSSE FUN FACTS

1. The game was first played by the Algonquin and Iroquois peoples in the St. Lawrence Valley of the United States and Canada.

2. Lacrosse was originally created for warrior training.

3. The original field of play for Native Americans could be as large as the distance between villages with no boundaries. However, the Iroquois often played on a field of 500 yards.

4. In 1636, Jean de Brebeuf, a French Jesuit missionary, wrote about a game he watched the indigenous Hurons play and named it "lacrosse." The "cross" is the stick with the net pocket!

5. Modern lacrosse can be played outdoors (field lacrosse) or indoors (box lacrosse). Teams can be men's, women's, or mixed (called intercrosse). Wheelchair lacrosse can be played as well!

GLOSSARY

Algonquin – A Native American tribe traditionally located around the St. Lawrence Valley and Great Lakes regions.

follow through – To complete a movement for maximum speed, skill, and/or accuracy.

Huron – A Native American tribe traditionally located around the northeastern United States.

indigenous – Native to a certain place.

Iroquois – A Native American tribe traditionally located around the eastern United States.

roster – A list of names for a team.

ANSWERS

1. c   2. b   3. c   4. a   5. d   6. c   7. b   8. a   9. d   10. c

ONLINE RESOURCES

Booklinks
NONFICTION NETWORK
FREE! ONLINE NONFICTION RESOURCES

To learn more about lacrosse, self-reliance, and bullying visit **abdobooklinks.com**. These links are routinely monitored and updated to provide the most current information available.